Helen Greiner

Cofounder of the iRobot Corporation

Other titles in the Innovators series include:

Helen Greiner

Cofounder of the iRobot Corporation

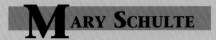

MARY SCHULTE

KIDHAVEN PRESS
A part of Gale, Cengage Learning

GALE
CENGAGE Learning·

Detroit • New York • San Francisco • New Haven, Conn • Waterville, Maine • London

LIBRARY OF CONGRESS CATALOGING-IN-PUBLICATION DATA

Schulte, Mary, 1958-
  Helen Greiner : cofounder of the iRobot Corporation / by Mary Schulte.
     p. cm. -- (Innovators)
  Includes bibliographical references and index.
  ISBN 978-0-7377-4404-0 (hardcover)
  1. Greiner, Helen, 1967---Juvenile literature. 2. Mechanical engineers--United States--Biography--Juvenile literature. 3. Inventors--United States--Biography--Juvenile literature. I. Title.
  TJ140.G74S345 2009
  629.8'92092--dc22
  [B]
                                                                    2009013446

KidHaven Press
27500 Drake Rd.
Farmington Hills, MI 48331

ISBN-13: 978-0-7377-4404-0
ISBN-10: 0-7377-4404-9

Printed in the United States of America
1 2 3 4 5 6 7 13 12 11 10 09

CONTENTS

Creator of Everyday Robots

The word *robot* often makes people think of a metallic, humanlike figure that moves stiffly with arms and legs, just like people. Actually, any mechanical device that performs tasks automatically or by remote control can be called a robot, or "bot." Robots come in many shapes and sizes. Some miniRobots are no bigger than a nickel, while other robots fill a whole room. Robots are programmed with computer instructions called **algorithms**.

Helen Greiner is a leader in designing and making robots. In 1990 she cofounded iRobot Corporation, a company that makes robots. Greiner was president of iRobot from 1997 to 2008 and chairman from 2005 to 2008. Today she is a member of the board, helping to oversee the operations of the company. iRobot created the most popular robot available for sale in stores, a **self-propelled** vacuum called the Roomba. iRobot also makes robots for the United States military. One called PackBot has been especially successful. It is a small, tanklike robot that can be used in areas too dangerous for soldiers.

Ever since she was a little girl, Greiner dreamed of creating robots. Her dreams came true when she and a college buddy, Colin Angle, and their professor, Rodney Brooks, started iRobot Corporation. Their goal has always been to make robots that touch people's everyday lives. A banner at the company head-quarters in Bedford, Massachusetts, displays their motto. It says, "Build cool stuff, deliver great products, make money, have fun and change the world."

Helen Greiner, chairman and cofounder of the iRobot Corporation, poses with an iRobot PackBot EOD in May 2005. iRobot created the Roomba vacuum and also makes robots for the United States military.

Greiner and her partners built iRobot from a company based in Angle's living room to a $257-million business with offices in Massachusetts, the District of Columbia, California, and Hong Kong and hundreds of employees. "We have built robots that go deep into the bore of oil wells, toys, museum displays, a **prototype** planetary explorer, a legged robot for underwater mines, a robotic fish, a **swarm** of 100 robots, and a robot that explored shafts in the great pyramid,"[1] Greiner said. When Greiner was chairman, she pushed the company toward creating more robots to perform everyday tasks. These robots would help people with dirty, boring, and difficult jobs.

Greiner predicts a future where robotic assistants will make life easier. "In ten years, I believe every house with a PC [personal computer] will have not just one but several robots for time-consuming chores," Greiner said. "Envision robots taking on the dusting, cleaning bathrooms, cleaning pools, mowing lawns, washing windows as well as reminding you to take your medication, bringing you a drink, and more."[2]

CHAPTER 1

A Fascination with Robots

Helen Greiner was born in London, England, on December 6, 1967. Greiner's father was from Hungary. He left his country in 1956 and went to London. He met Greiner's mother at the University of London where they both attended school.

Greiner may have inherited her keen interest in science and technology from her parents. Her mother taught math and science. Her father studied chemistry in school and became a businessman.

When Greiner was five years old, her family moved to the United States. She grew up in Southampton, New York, a suburb of New York City.

Falling in Love with a Robot

In 1977, when Greiner was ten years old, she went to the movie theater to see *Star Wars*. She was spellbound by the 3-foot-tall (0.9m) **android** named R2D2. Her fascination with the me-

Helen Greiner first became interested in robots when she saw R2D2 in *Star Wars*.

chanical creature sparked her lifelong interest in robots.

"I was enthralled by R2D2 because he was more than a machine," she recalled. "He was a character, he had a personality and he was really one of the stars of the show."[3]

At the time, Greiner thought she was watching a real robot zoom across the screen. Her older brother broke the news that the little robot that beeped and whirred was actually a small man inside a plastic costume. Greiner was disappointed, but not discouraged. She promised herself she would some day make a real robot.

Budding Young Scientist

From a young age, Greiner loved science and engineering. Her big brother had electronic toys, and radio-controlled cars. They were typical toys for boys, but Greiner wanted them, too. Sometimes she was so envious, she just took his toys.

When Greiner's family bought a computer, she latched onto it. She sat in front of it for hours, experimenting and learning how it worked. Soon she figured out how to program the computer to control the remote control toys.

"At the time, I was hacking on a computer, a TRS-80 that my parents had bought for the family," she said. "I could see the connection between what was shown in science fiction, in *Star Wars*, and what could be built in the future with technologies that were just emerging for the computer industry."[4]

Greiner joined the chess team and math team in high school. Her interest in computers and robots continued to grow. She was determined to study robotics, even though few women worked in the robot industry at that time. After graduating from high school, she attended the Massachusetts Institute of

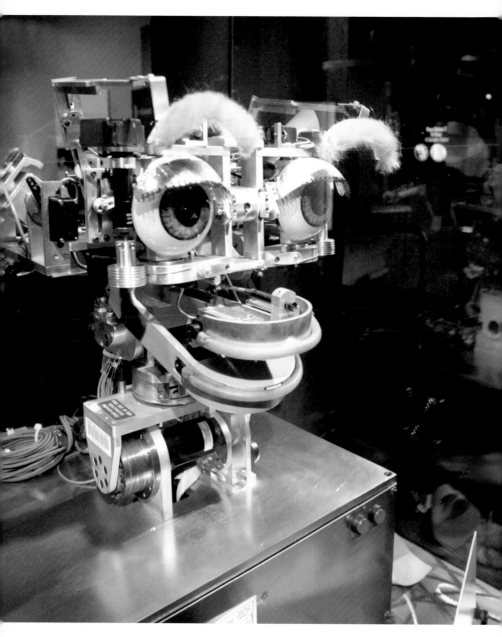

Kismet, a robot operated by the Massachusetts Institute of Technology's Artificial Intelligence Laboratory from 1993 to 2000, appears on display at the MIT Museum. Greiner received her bachelor's and master's degrees from MIT.

Technology (MIT) in Cambridge, Massachusetts, where she studied for a mechanical engineering degree. Greiner focused her studies on robotics and **artificial intelligence**.

Like Minds at MIT

Greiner met her future business partners while attending MIT in the late 1980s. She immediately bonded with classmate Colin Angle, who also dedicated his time to studying robots. Greiner and Angle discovered they shared another interest, too—snowboarding. In between classes, Greiner worked in MIT's Artificial Intelligence Laboratory. Her other future business partner, Professor Rodney Brooks, was in charge of the lab.

Greiner took a break from classes at MIT and went to Pasadena, California, where she **interned** at the Jet Propulsion Lab at the National Aeronautics and Space Administration. She worked on space satellites and helped design robots to do re-

iRobot cofounders Helen Greiner and Colin Angle met at MIT in the late 1980s. Both Greiner and Angle enjoyed studying robots.

pairs in space. Greiner then returned to MIT, and in 1989 she completed her bachelor's degree in mechanical engineering. A year later she earned her master's degree in computer science, also from MIT.

Greiner's first job after earning her degrees was with a company called California Cybernetics, in California. She worked on robots that help build cars. The company also focused on developing jet propulsion technology and on robot research. Within a year, her buddy Angle called. He asked if she would team up with him to create a robotics company. Greiner packed her bags and returned to Massachusetts the next day.

Greiner and Angle teamed up with Brooks and launched a robot company called IS Robotics in Somerville, a city near Boston, Massachusetts. Each of the partners took a leading role. Greiner became president of the company; Angle was the chief executive officer; and Brooks was chief technology officer. Greiner and her partners really believed in their company. With little money to get their company started, they established their headquarters in Angle's living room. They hired six employees to help design and build the robots and sometimes also brought in MIT students to work as interns.

A Tough Start for IS Robotics

Robot technology followed a path similar to most new technologies when they are first introduced. The first robots were expensive. They often cost tens of thousands of dollars and were used only in scientific research and industry.

Greiner, Angle, and Brooks wanted to change that. They planned to create robots that improved people's lives. Their biggest challenge was to make robots that would be affordable. If **consumers** could not afford the robots, they would not buy them.

For eight years, they sold robots to colleges, research labs, and government agencies while they worked on new ideas for robots that would help people with everyday tasks. Each robot sold for about $3,000, but they sold only about 60 robots per year and parts were expensive. The partners worked eighteen-hour days, but they were not making a profit. The

MIT professor Rodney Brooks was the chief technology officer of IS Robotics. Greiner, Angle, and Brooks wanted to create robots that would improve people's lives and were also affordable.

team had to take out loans of more than $100,000 to keep the company going.

The young company faced a lot of challenges. On one early project, Greiner, Angle, and Brooks were trying to meet an important deadline. They worked until 3 A.M. on the due date, trying to complete the robot. Before they could finish, something went terribly wrong and the robot burst into flames. Greiner learned from their unfortunate experience that she had two wonderful business partners. Realizing there was nothing they could do that night and the delivery would be late, they laughed at their bad luck and went out to breakfast. The next day they began to rebuild.

CHAPTER 2

Hard-Working Robots

Although Helen Greiner and her partners wanted to create robots for the public, their first big successes were with government projects. In 1993 the Defense Department and the Office of Naval Research asked IS Robotics to design a robot that could locate mines, especially underwater mines.

The IS engineers came up with a clever design. They made a robot that is like a ghost crab, a real **crustacean** that lives on beaches and can crawl along the ocean floor. They called the robot Ariel Underwater. Ariel even looked a little like a crab. It had a flat, square body with six legs coming out from the sides. The six-legged robot moved back and forth with the tides as it clutched the ocean floor, just like a real ghost crab. Ariel could locate mines placed underwater and in the ground.

The success of the Ariel project gave IS Robotics a financial boost. The partners decided it was time to move out of Angle's

living room and into new headquarters. They added more employees and also changed the company name.

Isaac Asimov and the Three Laws of Robotics

Greiner decided she wanted a more personal name for the company. So the partners changed it from IS Robotics to iRobot. The
name comes from a book about robots. Isaac Asimov published
the futuristic story *I, Robot* in 1950. Asimov is a popular Ameri-
can science-fiction author who wrote many books and short
stories. He created the term *robotics*. He also developed what he
called the Three Laws of Robotics. They are:

1. A robot may not harm or injure a human being.

2. A robot must obey the orders that a human being
   gives to it, unless it would result in injury.

3. A robot must protect its
   own existence as long
   as it does not interfere
   with laws number one
   or two.[5]

Greiner loved Asimov's
ideas when she read his stories
in high school. For her, "iRobot" seemed like the perfect

**In 1950 Isaac Asimov pub-
lished the futuristic story *I,
Robot*. This story inspired
Greiner to change the name of
her company to iRobot.**

name for a robotics company. She said, "First, for the **technophiles**, it is the name of Isaac Asimov's futuristic book. Second, it combines one (the personal) with robots (the technology). It can also be thought of as interactive, intelligent, interconnected Robots."[6]

PackBot Joins the Army

In 1995 the Defense Department hired iRobot to make another robot to help soldiers with dangerous tasks. iRobot built PackBot, a small robot that has interchangeable parts so it can help with many different tasks. It can defuse bombs, explore unknown areas, search buildings, and carry supplies. PackBot moves on tanklike tracks. The tracks can flip in a complete circle, so the PackBot can climb stairs and steep inclines. It can travel over rough ground and turn itself upright if it gets knocked over. PackBot became one of iRobot's most successful products.

PackBots were sent on an unexpected mission in 2001. After the September 11, 2001, terrorist attack on the World Trade Center in New York, four PackBots were used to evaluate the safety of buildings nearby. A year later PackBots were sent on their first combat mission. The army sent **surveillance** and security PackBots to the war in Afghanistan. Their job was to search for booby traps using cameras and sensors. They also searched caves for terrorists. PackBots were also sent to Iraq in 2003. They searched for mines and booby traps in vehicles, airfields, and buildings.

PackBots can destroy bombs and they can also pick up a bomb and move it. They have carried out thousands of bomb-disposal missions. In most missions, the PackBot returns

Greiner demonstrates a PackBot, a robot that can help soldiers defuse bombs, explore unknown areas, and perform other dangerous tasks.

safely, but sometimes it is blown up, which is why the army likes to use robots instead of people for this dangerous work.

The Warrior

iRobot's latest military robot, called the Warrior, could be the PackBot's big brother. It is a 250-pound (113kg) robot that can haul cargo and move over almost any type of terrain, including stairs. It can climb steeper hills and carry more weight than Pack-Bot. The Warrior can carry an injured soldier from the battlefield,

move heavy debris, carry supplies such as firefighting gear, and detonate or disarm bombs.

The Warrior can move 12 miles per hour (19kmph). It can also take supplies and ammunition to soldiers pinned down by enemy fire.

A Robot at the Great Pyramid

iRobot developed a reputation for creating great robots. The company's robots could scale walls, squeeze through narrow

pipes, even drill through stone. In the summer of 2002, iRobot was asked to build a robot to explore a pyramid that had been sealed for 4,500 years.

The Great Pyramid of Giza, located near Cairo, Egypt, was built around 2650 B.C. by the Egyptian pharaoh Khufu for his burial tomb. Made of more than 2 million stone blocks and containing a few different chambers and four narrow shafts leading away from the chambers, it is one of the largest pyramids ever built. There is a central shaft

iRobot's latest military robot is called the Warrior, a 250-pound robot that can haul cargo, remove injured soldiers from the battlefield, and act as a demolition expert.

that researchers think might have been designed for religious reasons because it points toward the star Sirius and the constellation Orion. The National Geographic Society and Egypt's Supreme Council of Antiquities asked iRobot to build a robot to explore two shafts that lead away from a room called the queen's chamber. One of the shafts was blocked with what looked like a small door. Researchers wanted to know what lay beyond the door.

iRobot accepted the challenge to build a robot to explore the shafts. First, the iRobot engineers built a scale model of the shaft so they could study its angle, height, and width. Then they built the Pyramid Rover. It took six months and cost $250,000 to build the small robot that measured approximately 5 inches by 11 inches (12.7cm by 27.9cm). It expanded and contracted in height from 4 to 11 inches (10.2cm to 27.9cm). This allowed the rover to move steadily by gripping the top and the bottom of the shaft.

The Great Pyramid of Giza is the site of an exploration project involving an iRobot product.

Pavlo Rudakevych (left) and Gregg Landry work with the Pyramid Rover, a robot designed to explore a small air shaft that leads away from a room called the queen's chamber inside the Great Pyramid of Giza.

The rover carried a light, a **gauge**, a drill, and a tiny camera. When it reached the blockage, it measured the thickness of the rock with the gauge. The rover then drilled a tiny hole through the stone. Using its extension arm, the rover inserted a tiny camera through the hole. Millions of people watched the live broadcast on the Fox television network and also on the National Geographic Channel to see what lay on the other side of the door.

Researchers had hoped they might find a chamber filled with treasures, such as those found in Tutankhamen's tomb. But rover showed a small, empty chamber blocked by another small door. Although no treasures were found, iRobot's Pyramid Rover performed its job perfectly.

CHAPTER 3

A Robot for
Every Home

According to the Robotics Industries Association, there are 182,000 commercial robots in use in the United States. Many of them work in the automotive industry, spraying paint and welding. Only Japan uses more commercial robots.

Helen Greiner and her partners knew their engineers could make many types of robots. They asked themselves, what kind of robot would people want to buy?

A Toy Robot

In 1998 the Hasbro toy company gave iRobot $1 million to complete development of a doll called My Real Baby. The doll responded to a child's touch through sensors. A motor moved the doll's skin, so it could frown, smile, and scrunch up its face. It also laughed, cried, sucked its thumb, and made baby sounds. The doll could say simple words and phrases, such as *mama* and *night-night*. My Real Baby cost $95.95 when it went on sale in 2000.

In 1998 iRobot and Hasbro teamed up to produce My Real Baby, the first interactive doll to respond to a child's actions with such realistic responses as smiling, frowning, and sucking its thumb.

My Real Baby's features were not enough to make it a popular toy, and it did not sell well. iRobot stopped production of the doll after only about 100,000 of the dolls had been made. Some critics said the price was just too high. iRobot still considered the doll a success, because it had finally built a robot that interacted with regular people.

iRobot Courts Investors

iRobot wanted to make more products and expand distribution, but it needed money to grow. It decided to ask venture capitalists for the money. Venture capitalists are people who invest money in new companies. Greiner did not have time to ask venture capitalists individually for money, so she spoke to several hundred of them at once in a forum at MIT.

One by one, about 30 presenters talked about their products during the forum. Greiner was the last speaker. As she waited, Greiner sent the company's robotic vacuum rolling around the conference room. By the time she talked about her company, the disc-shaped vacuum had charmed investors. One of the investors, Trident Capital, invested $9 million to help iRobot bring their robotic vacuum to market.

Engineers had worked for twelve years to perfect the vacuum design. They spent many hours studying how to clean floors. Designers actually spent one night at a department store to watch cleaners at work. In 2002, with help from the $9-million investment, iRobot released its robotic vacuum—the Roomba.

The Roomba is a round, 5-pound (2.2kg), 13-inch-wide (33cm) automated vacuum. It uses an advanced navigation system to clean household floors, such as carpet, wood, tile, and linoleum. It needs no human supervision and it runs on re-

In 2002 iRobot released the Roomba, which is an automated vacuum. The Roomba's unique advanced navigation technology allows it to clean all household floor surfaces, including carpet, tile, wood, and linoleum.

chargeable batteries. One of the advanced models is designed to maneuver into its charging dock and plug itself in to recharge.

A Smart Little Robot

When the Roomba hit the market in 2002, *Time* magazine, *Business Week*, and *USA Today* called it one of the year's best products. More than 2.5 million Roombas, each costing $150 to $300, have been sold since its debut. The Roomba is the most successful mobile robot ever made.

"These are really, really smart little devices," said Greiner. "You just push a button and you can check vacuuming off your to-do list."[7]

"I just love gardening," Greiner says. "I spend a lot of time putting flowers in my house and making an English wildflower garden. Which is why things like the Roomba are so invaluable. If I'm at home, I don't want to spend time vacuuming or washing my kitchen floor. I want to spend time out doing the gardening."[8]

Some people treat their Roomba as a pet, even naming it. Greiner called her first Roomba "Arnie" after the *Terminator* movie character played by Arnold Schwarzenegger.

Hacking a Roomba

Some people like the Roomba because they can reprogram it to do other tasks. One person made it into a webcam on wheels that he can control through the Internet. Someone else made it into a plant-mover system, so the plants are always in the sun.

There is even a Web site where people discuss modifications to their Roombas. The site is not run by iRobot, but the company is aware of it. "When I was in junior high school, I was hacking on a computer system," Greiner says. "Kids don't hack computers now because they come as turn-key products and they already have all this great software running on them. But kids are hacking robots and learning about technology by opening up and tinkering with robot systems."[9] It is all part of the learning process with robots.

The Scooba and the Dirt Dog

iRobot also makes a floor-scrubbing robot called the Scooba. It maps a room by following walls or bouncing off of them. The robot's software tracks its movements in circles and lines so it can clean an entire area.

Nancy Dussault (right) from the iRobot Corporation spills coffee to show trade show attendees how the Scooba works. The robot washes, scrubs, and dries floors.

Inside the Scooba, a mop dunks into a bucket of water. Jets spray a mixture of water and cleaning fluid (or water and white vinegar) on the floor. A squeegee sucks up the liquid and vacuums it into a water tank.

Like the Roomba and the Scooba, the Dirt Dog works on its own, but it has more power to suck up things, like wood chips and metal shavings. Brushes inside the Dirt Dog spin at 1,000 revolutions per minute, dumping the mess into a larger disposal bin.

iRobot now provides a self-propelled cleaning robot for every type of floor space in an average home. The Roomba cleans carpets and floors; the Scooba mops tile, wood, and linoleum floors; and the Dirt Dog sweeps garages and basements.

The ConnectR

One of the newest robots in development at iRobot is a **virtual** visit robot called the ConnectR. Using audio, video, and remote controls, it allows people in different places to see and hear each other. Pet owners can use it to check on their pets. Users could be parents at work who want to see and speak with their children who are at home. ConnectR could also be used to check in with elderly family members.

"Imagine a version [of ConnectR] in an elderly relative's house," Greiner said. "You could log in and visit with them anytime, from anywhere. And then, maybe it could start to help them more and more on its own—finding misplaced glasses or fetching medicines."[10]

The engineers at iRobot worked on ConnectR for many years. A version of the virtual visiting bot was sent to a small group of consumers for **beta testing** in 2007. After beta testing iRobot decided not to release ConnectR to the general public. The company is making some changes to it, based on the testers' feedback and has not announced a new release date.

A Future with Robots

Greiner says it is difficult to make accurate predictions about technology too far into the future. She has no doubt, however, that robots will change industries. From oil production to cleaning to mining, robots will bring changes.

Greiner predicts that almost every home in the United States will have a robot to do housecleaning and babysitting one day. She wants to get robots out of research labs and into real people's hands. She says, "Robots will be cleaning floors and acting as remote eyes and ears. Within 15 years, they will work as true personal assistants and friends."[11]

CHAPTER 4

Encouraging Women in Technology

Helen Greiner works mostly with men. Traditionally, more men than women pursue robotics careers. Greiner works with educators to change this, to encourage girls to consider careers in mechanical engineering. Greiner says it is important to show young people, especially girls, all of the jobs that are available.

"Girls think [engineering is] geeky, but it's so creative and interesting," Greiner said. "You can build a bridge or a robot or a new computer system."[12]

The great thing about robotics, Greiner says, is that the field is still young. New ideas pop up often. Engineers have the chance to experiment.

"Engineering is a great field for women," Greiner said. "Building a robot allows you to use your imagination and gives you a sense of accomplishment and empowerment, because you can see your creation 'come to life.' What's cooler than that?"[13]

Excelling in a Man's Field

When Greiner was young, she was not encouraged to pursue a career in technology. At that time, people did not think of it as a field for women.

Greiner proved them wrong. She not only jumped into robotics, but she also rose to the top. People might have thought Greiner would focus mostly on iRobot's consumer products, like the robotic baby doll, the vacuum, and the floor mopper, but she also worked on military projects. Greiner

Helen Greiner enjoys working on iRobot's military projects. Here, she speaks during a demonstration of life-saving military robots.

enjoyed talking with the soldiers and generals to learn what robotic equipment would help them on the battlefield.

Greiner says women bring special skills to running a company. "Building teams, solving problems, and juggling many things at once are things that women do very well, and things that corporate executives need to do to be successful."[14]

As a woman in a leadership role, Greiner points out that her success can be traced to the struggles of other women. She appreciates the generations of women before her who made sacrifices to give women equal opportunities.

Awards for Greiner

Greiner has received many awards and honors over the years. In 2000 she won the prestigious DemoGod Award, which recognized her pioneering efforts in consumer and industrial robotics.

In 2002 MIT's *Technology Review* named Greiner one of the world's 100 Top Young Innovators. The next year she was recognized by *Fortune* magazine as one of the Top 10 Innovators in the United States. She also won the Ernst and Young New England Entrepreneur of the Year (with her partner Colin Angle) and was a National Award Nominee.

Good Housekeeping magazine named Greiner Entrepreneur of the Year in 2005. Greiner was inducted into the Women in Technology International Hall of Fame in 2007.

The Anita Borg Institute for Women and Technology hosted its third annual Women of Vision Awards banquet on May 8, 2008. They honored three leaders in technology, including Greiner in the Innovation category. In her acceptance speech, Greiner said that even though she demonstrated all the signs of being a geek growing up, no one encouraged her to think about

Helen Greiner and Colin Angle celebrate as one of their company's PackBot robots opens on Nasdaq in November 2005. Greiner has received many awards and honors throughout her career.

becoming an engineer. She stressed that it is important to encourage kids early in life, to increase **innovation** in the future.

Greiner Looks Ahead

Greiner's role at iRobot evolved over the years. At first, she worked with engineering, helping to design and build robots.

Then, as chairperson, she looked to the future of the company, providing vision and guiding development of a wide variety of robots that would help the company succeed. In 2008 Greiner resigned from iRobot. Now she is the president of the Robotics Technology Consortium, a national organization of about 90 robot companies.

Greiner expects to continue to work in robot technology. She says, "I am a robot person and I've been a robot person all my life, since I was 11. I was enthralled with R2D2, and I've wanted to build robots ever since. Once robots grab you, you're kind of hooked."[15]

NOTES

Introduction: Creator of Everyday Robots

1. Quoted in Phillip Torrone, "Interview: Helen Greiner, Chairman and Cofounder of iRobot, Corp.," *Engadget.com*, August 2, 2004, http://features.engadget.com/2004/08/02/interview-helen-greiner-chairman-and-cofounder-of-irobot.

2. Quoted in Erik Rhey, "Q&A: iRobot Co-Founder Helen Greiner," *PCMag.com*, April 18, 2007, www.pcmag.com/article2/0,2817,2113988,00.asp.

Chapter One: A Fascination with Robots

3. Quoted in *Knowledge@Wharton*, "Is There a Robot in Your Future? Helen Greiner Thinks So," *Knowledge@Wharton*, June 2, 2006, http://knowledge.wharton.upenn.edu/article.cfm?articleid=1435.

4. Quoted in *Knowledge@Wharton*, "Is There a Robot in Your Future?"

Chapter Two: Hard-Working Robots

5. Isaac Asimov, *I, Robot*. New York: Bantam Dell, 1950, pp. 44–45.

6. Quoted in Deepa Kandaswamy, "Queen of Robotics," *Dataquest*, March 17, 2004, http://dqindia.ciol.com/content/industrymarket/datatalk/2004/104031701.asp.

Chapter Three: A Robot for Every Home

7. Quoted in Tara Kimura, "Domestic Helpers?" *CBC News*, July 7, 2007, www.cbc.ca/news/background/tech/robotics/domestic-helpers.html.

8. Quoted in *Knowledge@Wharton*. "Is there a Robot in your Future?"

9. Quoted in *Knowledge@Wharton*. "Is there a Robot in your Future?"

10. Quoted in Kandaswamy, "Queen of Robotics."

11. Quoted in Robert Buderi, "Helen Greiner Speaks: Next Up After iRobot Is Service, Kite-Boarding, and Gearing up for a New Adventure . . . in Robotics," *Xconomy*, October 22, 2008, www.xconomy.com/boston/2008/10/22/helen-greiner-speaks-next-up-after-irobot-is-service-kite-boarding-and-gearing-up-for-a-new-adventurein-robotics.

Chapter Four: Encouraging Women in Technology

12. Quoted in Rhey, "Q&A: iRobot Co-Founder Helen Greiner."

13. Quoted in Deepa Kandaswamy, "Personality, Future Zone," *Hindu*, August 22, 2004, www.hinduonnet.com/thehindu/mag/2004/08/22/stories/2004082200400500.htm.

14. Robert Buderi, "iRobot Founder To Be Inducted into Women's Technology Hall of Fame," *Xconomy*, September 5, 2007, www.xconomy.com/2007/09/05/irobot-founder-to-be-inducted-into-womens-technology-hall-of-fame.

15. Quoted in Buderi, "Helen Greiner Speaks."

GLOSSARY

algorithms: A set of mathematical instructions that must be followed in a specific order to answer a mathematical problem.

android: A robot made to look like a human.

artificial intelligence: The study of how to produce machines that work like the human mind, with the ability to understand language, solve problems, and learn.

beta testing: A last test for a computer product before it is available for sale.

consumers: People who buy goods or services for their own use.

crustacean: An animal that lives in water and has a hard outer shell.

gauge: A device for measuring the amount or size of something.

innovation: A new idea or method.

interned: Trained for a skilled job by performing work, usually with little or no pay.

prototype: The first version of something, such as a machine.

self-propelled: Moves by its own power.

surveillance: Careful watching of a person or place.

swarm: A large group all moving together.

technophiles: People who are enthusiastic about new technology.

virtual: Something that can be done or seen or heard using a computer, making it unnecessary to physically be there.

FOR FURTHER EXPLORATION

Book

Isaac Asimov, *I, Robot*. New York: Bantam Dell, 1950. A collection of stories about robots.

Internet Sources

Nancy Gupton, "Ancient Egyptian Chambers Explored," *National Geographic News*, April 4, 2003, http://news.nationalgeographic.com/news/2002/09/0910_020913_egypt_1.html.

Margaret Heffernan, "Robot Inventor Helen Greiner," *Reader'sDigest.com*, September 2008, www.rd.com/your-america-inspiring-people-and-stories/robot-inventor-helen-greiner/article96752.html.

Knowledge@Wharton, "Is There a Robot in Your Future? Helen Greiner Thinks So," *Knowledge@Wharton*, April 5, 2006, http://knowledge.wharton.upenn.edu/article.cfm?articleid=1435.

Web Site

iRobot (www.irobot.com). This is the official Web site of the company cofounded by Helen Greiner.

INDEX

PICTURE CREDITS

ABOUT THE AUTHOR

Mary Schulte is a children's author and newspaper photo editor in Kansas City, Missouri. She has written twelve nonfiction books, including *Sirens* and *Minotaur* in KidHaven Press's Monsters series. She has three children, three dogs, two cats, and a very busy Roomba.